# THE DREAMER'S ABYSS

## "A JOURNEY THROUGH THE FRACTURED MIND"

## SUNIL K

Made with ♥ on the Notion Press Platform
www.notionpress.com

To Stewart, who wandered through the abyss but never
lost himself.
To Melissa and James, who waited in the waking world.
And to the dream itself—for revealing more than reality
ever could.

# Contents

# Foreword

Dreams have fascinated humanity for as long as we have been able to sleep. They are fleeting, vivid, and sometimes more real than the waking world itself. But what happens when dreams refuse to let go? When the boundary between consciousness and illusion blurs, and a person is trapped in a place where time bends, reality shifts, and escape seems impossible?

The Dreamer's Abyss is a journey into that uncertainty. At its heart, this story follows Stewart, a young man suffering from Kleine-Levin Syndrome, a rare condition that plunges him into prolonged episodes of sleep. But what should have been a temporary descent into unconsciousness becomes something far more sinister—a world where he must fight to survive, unravel the truth of his existence, and ultimately decide whether waking up is truly the goal.

This novel explores the fragility of perception, the terror of being lost in one's own mind, and the question of whether we are ever truly awake. It is a tale for those who have questioned their own reality, for those who have found solace in dreams, and for those who fear what lurks just beyond their understanding.

As you turn the pages, remember: not all dreams are meant to end.

Welcome to The Dreamer's Abyss.

# Preface

This story began with a conversation. My friend and I were discussing lucid dreaming—the idea of being fully aware and in control within a dream. At first, it was just curiosity, a fascinating concept that felt like an escape from reality. But the more we talked, the more I realized something: dreams and reality are not as separate as we think. Our waking life is just as unpredictable, shaped by fears, anxieties, and the narratives we create in our minds. Sometimes, we are more trapped in our thoughts than in any dream.

From that discussion, The Dreamer's Abyss was born—not just as a story of dreams, but as a reflection of the psychological battles we all fight. Stewart's journey is not just about being lost in a surreal, shifting world; it is about the weight of our fears, the way we amplify small worries into overwhelming terrors, and how that inner chaos disturbs everything around us. In many ways, we are all trapped in our own versions of Stewart's dream, spiraling deeper into anxieties we create for ourselves.

Kleine-Levin Syndrome gave me the perfect framework—a real-world disorder where people experience prolonged sleep episodes, disconnected from time and reality. But the heart of this novel is not just about being asleep. It's about the struggle to wake up—not just physically, but emotionally and mentally. It's about learning to separate what is real from what our fears make us believe.

This book is for those who have ever felt lost in their own mind, for those who have fought against their own thoughts, and for those who seek the courage to break free.

The battle is not just in the dream—it is in us.
   —Sunil K

# Acknowledgements

No story is written in isolation, and The Dreamer's Abyss would not have been possible without the support, inspiration, and encouragement of many people.

First, I want to thank my friend, whose deep conversations about lucid dreaming and the blurred lines between reality and illusion sparked the very idea of this novel. Those discussions led me down a path of exploration—not just into dreams, but into the fragile nature of the human mind itself.

I am deeply grateful for the support, ideas, and suggestions given to us during the writing of this book. A special thanks to our teachers, whose guidance and feedback helped refine and shape this story into what it is today.

A huge thanks to Google for being an endless source of knowledge and to all the individuals who have shared valuable information about Kleine-Levin Syndrome and dream psychology on the internet. Your contributions helped shape the foundation of this book, making Stewart's journey more authentic and deeply human.

To every reader who picks up this book, thank you for stepping into this abyss with me. This story now belongs to you, and I hope it makes you question, reflect, and perhaps even see your own dreams a little differently.

Finally, to the dreamers, the wanderers, and those who fight unseen battles within their own minds—this book is for you.

—Sunil K

# Prologue

Stewart had always been a quiet observer of the world. Not withdrawn, but never quite present either—like someone standing at the edge of a conversation, listening but never speaking. His mind was a restless place, filled with thoughts that never seemed to settle, worries that grew larger the longer he held onto them.

His parents, Melissa and James, had always tried to understand him. His mother, gentle but firm, would often remind him not to let his thoughts consume him. His father, ever pragmatic, believed most problems had solutions if one only looked hard enough. Stewart wasn't sure if that was true. Some problems felt too big to solve.

Lately, he had been feeling... strange. More distant than usual. Conversations would slip past him as if he were hearing them from underwater. He had chalked it up to exhaustion, the stress of school, the endless weight of expectations pressing down on him.

That night, as he lay in bed, staring at the ceiling, he felt it again—that strange heaviness in his limbs, the fog creeping into his mind.

He barely registered the sound of his mother calling his name from the other room.

And then, he slept

# 1

# The Awakening and the Unknown

---

The first thing Stewart noticed was the smell—sharp, sterile, laced with something artificial that made his stomach turn. Then came the light, pressing against his closed eyelids, too bright, too harsh. A steady, rhythmic beeping filled the air, impersonal and distant. Something was wrong.

His fingers twitched against stiff sheets, and the sound of movement stirred beside him. He forced his eyes open, blinking against the blinding whiteness. A hospital room. The realization came slow, sluggish, like wading through water.

Melissa sat by his bedside, her hands clasped tightly in her lap, knuckles pale. She looked exhausted—more than exhausted. James stood by the window, arms crossed, his gaze fixed outside, his jaw set in a way Stewart knew meant he was trying to hold something back.

Something about their expressions sent an uneasy chill through him.

"Mom?" His voice cracked, dry as sandpaper.

Melissa startled, then exhaled sharply, relief and worry tangled in her face. She reached for his hand, gripping it tight, as if reassuring herself that he was real. "Oh, sweetheart... you're awake." Her fingers trembled against his. "You're finally awake."

Stewart frowned, his brain sluggish. "Finally?" His throat burned as he swallowed. "How long?"

A silence stretched between them. His mother looked to his father, but James didn't turn from the window. It was the doctor who finally spoke.

"Thirteen days."

Stewart's stomach dropped. "What?"

"You've been asleep for nearly two weeks," the doctor repeated, his voice measured, as if easing into something worse. "Your parents brought you here after you wouldn't wake up. Your vitals remained stable, but we ran extensive tests to rule out infections, metabolic disorders, neurological conditions—"

"This is a joke, right?" Stewart cut in, his pulse spiking. "People don't just sleep for two weeks."

The doctor sighed, setting his clipboard aside. He was an older man, with silver at his temples and the kind of voice that had delivered bad news far too many times.

"Stewart," he said gently, "you have a condition called Kleine-Levin Syndrome."

Stewart blinked. The words didn't land at first. They floated in the space between them, meaningless, weightless. He was twenty-nine years old. How did someone go nearly three decades without knowing they had something like this?

"It's a rare neurological disorder," the doctor continued, his tone calm but firm. "Sometimes referred to as 'Sleeping Beauty Syndrome.' It causes recurring episodes of excessive sleep, altered perception, and cognitive disturbances. During these episodes, your awareness and memory may be impaired. When you wake up, you may not realize how much time has passed."

Stewart let out a short, disbelieving laugh. "You're kidding."

"I wish I were."

Melissa's grip tightened. "They... they don't know what triggers it," she said, her voice unsteady. "They said this might happen again. That it's—" She swallowed hard. "Episodic."

Episodic. As if his life would be split into fragments, whole weeks vanishing without warning.

Stewart tried to process it, but his thoughts felt scrambled, slipping through his fingers like sand. He searched his father's face for something—reassurance, maybe—but James was still staring out the window, his shoulders stiff, his expression unreadable.

A deep unease settled in Stewart's chest. Not just from the diagnosis, not just from the hospital walls pressing in on him. It was something else. A feeling. A hum at the edge of his consciousness, distant but growing.

He closed his eyes for a moment, exhaling slowly. But the second he did, something flickered in the darkness behind his eyelids—colours shifting, shapes stretching, a place that didn't belong.

His eyes snapped open.

No. Just exhaustion. Just shock.

But deep down, something in his gut twisted.

*What if it wasn't?*

His stomach growled suddenly, breaking the silence. He blinked, surprised by the hunger gnawing at his insides. "I haven't eaten in thirteen days," he muttered, rubbing his face. "God, can I get at least a burger before we start panicking?"

Melissa let out a choked laugh, half relief, half exasperation. Even James smirked slightly, finally turning from the window.

Stewart cracked a small grin, the weight in the room lifting—just a little.

# 2
# Back to Reality (Sort Of)

Stewart stood outside the hospital, squinting up at the overcast sky as if the clouds held answers. After a week of being poked, prodded, and pitied, he was finally free. Sort of. His body still felt like a borrowed suit, slightly off in the shoulders, too loose in the legs. He took a deep breath and stepped forward, wincing at the sudden dizziness. Yep. Definitely not at a hundred percent.

His father, James, insisted on driving him home, delivering his usual blend of concern and gruffness. "You sure you don't need another day off?"

"I need the paycheck more than I need my sanity," Stewart replied, staring out the window.

"That's not comforting."

"It wasn't meant to be."

James sighed but said nothing else, dropping Stewart off at his apartment. After a quick shower and a stale granola bar, he was back out the door, heading to work.

Stewart worked at a mid-sized tech company, a place where innovation allegedly thrived but was mostly drowned out by passive-aggressive emails and broken coffee machines. He had barely stepped into the office when a familiar voice greeted him.

"Look who decided to come back from his coma!" said Danny, his best work buddy and resident office menace. "We took bets. I had you down for at least another week."

"Glad to disappoint," Stewart muttered, tossing his bag onto his desk.

Danny leaned on the partition between their cubicles, grinning. "So, was it like Sleeping Beauty? Did a nurse have to kiss you awake? Or was it just your mom sobbing dramatically?"

"It was the beeping machines and my dad complaining about parking fees. Super romantic."

Danny snorted. "I knew it. No prince, no magic, just overpriced hospital coffee and your dad going, 'You know how much they charge per hour in that lot?'"

Stewart sighed. "He actually said that. Right after I woke up. My first words back to reality were, 'How much?'"

Danny clapped him on the shoulder. "Iconic. You should have milked it, though. Told them you saw the light. That you were floating through the clouds, then—bam!—hospital bill dragged you back to the mortal realm."

"I did try to act a little disoriented," Stewart admitted. "They just assumed that was my natural state."

Danny grinned. "Well, yeah. I mean, let's be honest, you always have that 'Did I just wake up?' look. I swear half the office thinks you're a malfunctioning robot trying to understand human behavior."

"You say that like it's a bad thing."

"Nah, it's charming. In a 'maybe he's possessed' kind of way."

A new voice joined the conversation—Susan. The Susan. The reason Stewart occasionally attempted hair gel and kept a spare breath mint in his pocket. "Hey, Stewart. Glad to see you're okay. We were worried."

Stewart turned, the witty response he had been preparing evaporating as soon as he met her green eyes. "Oh. Uh. Thanks. I mean, yeah. I mean—" He coughed, abandoning the sentence entirely.

Danny smirked. "We were just discussing his fairytale awakening. I bet it was a grumpy nurse."

"Oh, no way," Susan said with mock seriousness. "I think it was probably a dramatic gasp, then sitting bolt upright like Frankenstein."

"That... sounds about right," Stewart admitted, scratching the back of his head. "Except I also knocked over a water pitcher and nearly took out a nurse with a heart monitor cable."

Susan laughed, and Stewart would have happily been hit by another heart monitor just to hear that sound again.

Their manager, Mr. Davison, popped his head out of his office. "Stewart, good to see you back. Now, unless you're planning on charming your colleagues into doing your work for you, let's get to it."

Susan winked at Stewart before heading back to her desk, leaving him standing there like an idiot.

Danny elbowed him. "Dude. That was a prime flirting moment. You okay? Or did the coma wipe out your ability to function?"

"I was never functioning in the first place."

"Fair point."

Danny shook his head. "Listen, man. You need to step up your game. This is workplace romance gold right here. The tragic hero, back from the brink of death, trying to reclaim his lost time..."

"Lost time? I was gone for a week."

"A week in work years is like a decade. Legends have already formed. Some say you were training in a secret underground bunker. Others believe you discovered an ancient prophecy."

Stewart rolled his eyes. "Let me guess. You started all of those rumors?"

Danny grinned. "Maybe. But my personal favorite is the one where you woke up with amnesia and had to piece together your life through post-it notes and old Slack messages."

"That actually sounds more accurate than I'd like."

As Stewart sat down, booting up his computer, he tried to shake off the lingering fog in his brain. Something about waking up from this latest episode felt different. A shadow loomed in the depths of his mind, a whisper of something terrifying just beyond his grasp. The feeling gnawed at him, leaving a cold dread at the edge of his consciousness.

But then Danny leaned over with a smirk. "Oh, by the way, while you were out, I may have signed you up for the company talent show. You have three days to figure out if you juggle, dance, or embarrass yourself in front of Susan."

Stewart groaned. "No way, I can't."

Danny shrugged. "Only one way to find out. Welcome back, Sleeping Beauty."

And just like that, the horror in his mind took a backseat and he continued his office work.

# 3

## Fractured Nights

Stewart had always considered sleep a refuge. But as the final stretch of office hours ended and he returned home to his quiet apartment, sleep turned into something else—something darker, unpredictable. For the next few nights, he got a full eight hours, yet each time he closed his eyes, he entered a world that seemed determined to unearth every hidden crack in his life.

Stewart found himself at a dinner table—his childhood home, perfectly recreated. The scent of his mother's homemade lasagna filled the air, warm and inviting. His father sat at the head of the table, slicing bread, while his mother poured wine. His younger brother, Daniel, grinned at him from across the table. It felt... real. Too real.

Then, mid-sentence, his mother turned to him, her smile unwavering. "You shouldn't be here, Stewart."

His father continued slicing the bread. Except, the bread never ended. The slices curled, folded in on themselves, stacking endlessly into a growing tower of stale crusts.

"What do you mean?" Stewart asked, a strange unease settling into his chest.

Daniel chuckled. "You never belonged here."

Stewart tried to stand, but his legs wouldn't move. The chair had melted around him, gripping his thighs like wet clay. His mother reached for his hand—except her fingers elongated, stretching like vines, wrapping around his wrist, holding him in place. He gasped as her grip tightened, her face morphing into something hollow, her eyes empty sockets.

"You should leave us," she whispered, her voice warping, echoing like it came from a deep cave. "Before we leave you first."

He jolted awake, his chest heaving, sweat slicking his skin. The clock read 3:12 AM. The room was silent, but the dream clung to him, an eerie residue settling in his bones.

The next day, still unsettled, Stewart confided in his friend Danny over lunch. "These dreams... they feel too real. Like my mind's trying to tell me something."

Danny shrugged. "Maybe it is. If they keep messing with your head, take a break. Go somewhere for a few days. Get some space. Might help."

Stewart considered it, but that night, the dreams returned with even greater intensity.

The next night, Stewart was in a courtroom. His parents sat in the judge's seat, towering above him in oversized robes. The jury was filled with distorted versions of his relatives—faces stretched unnaturally long, eyes black pits of nothingness.

"You have been found guilty," his father declared, slamming a gavel down. The sound didn't stop—it kept echoing, growing louder until it turned into a heartbeat. His heartbeat.

"Wait—guilty of what?" Stewart demanded, standing at the defendant's podium, shackles suddenly clasped around his wrists.

His mother leaned forward, her lips curling in a grotesque smirk. "Of never belonging."

The floor cracked beneath him. He plunged into darkness, falling endlessly, until he hit the ground with a sickening thud.

When he looked up, his parents loomed over him, staring, unblinking. Their eyes weren't eyes anymore—just empty holes that swallowed everything.

A voice whispered from behind him, sending ice down his spine. "Run."

He turned, and everything went black.

He woke up gasping, his body trembling. His breaths came in short, uneven bursts. The room felt too small, too confined. He needed air. He needed space.

The dreams didn't stop. Every night, they twisted into new shapes—his mother laughing as she turned to dust in his hands, his father walking away without looking back, his childhood home crumbling as he stood outside, powerless. The message was always the same.

Leave.

By the morning of the fourth day, Stewart felt hollowed out. The anxiety clung to him even when he was awake, the echoes of his dreams whispering in the quiet moments.

He couldn't shake the feeling that he wasn't wanted—that maybe he never had been.

So he packed a bag.

That evening, he left, but not without a word. He placed a note on the dining table, explaining that he was going away, asking them not to follow. He also took leave from his office—an indefinite break from everything.

He headed to a remote mountain region, seeking solitude, distance. The cold air bit at his skin as he stepped into the small cabin he had rented. Finally, he was alone.

That night, as he lay in bed, silence pressed down on him. The darkness outside the window felt deeper than usual, stretching endlessly, as if the world beyond had disappeared.

Then—

A whisper. Not outside. Not in the wind.

Inside his mind.

"You're exactly where you need to be."

# 4

## The Descent into the Unseen

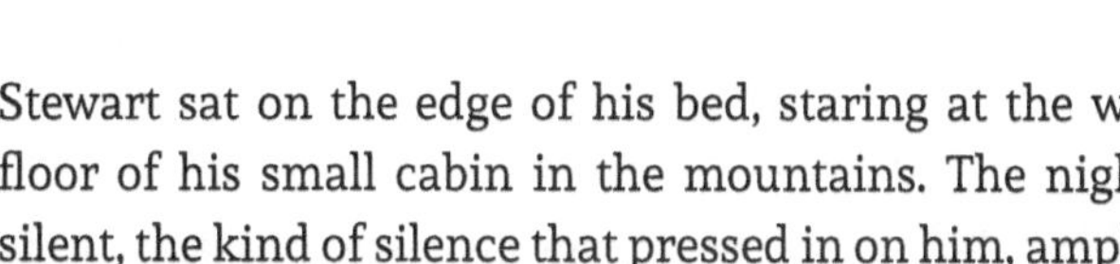

Stewart sat on the edge of his bed, staring at the wooden floor of his small cabin in the mountains. The night was silent, the kind of silence that pressed in on him, amplifying the distant whisper of wind through the trees. His fingers tapped restlessly against his knee. He had left home for peace, for solitude, yet his thoughts had only grown more restless.

His phone rang, the sudden vibration making him jolt. His heart lurched as he saw Danny's name flashing on the screen. He picked up immediately.

"Stewart, it's Susan," Danny's voice was strained, breathless. "She—she got hit by a car. We're on the way to the hospital."

The words slammed into him like a physical force. His breath caught in his throat. "What? Is she—?"

"I don't know, man. She's unconscious. Just get to the hospital."

Stewart didn't hesitate. He was already moving, shoving his feet into his boots and grabbing his jacket. His mind felt like it had been yanked from his body, thoughts rushing faster than he could process. He barely registered locking the cabin door before he was outside, the cold night air cutting against his skin.

The drive was a blur of headlights and empty roads. His grip on the wheel was tight, his knuckles white. His mind kept looping Danny's words. *She's unconscious.* His pulse roared in his ears, his thoughts spiraling between fear and urgency. He barely noticed when the road seemed to stretch longer than usual, the turns unfamiliar, but he chalked it up to adrenaline.

As he drove, his eyes caught something strange in the rearview mirror—his reflection seemed just a fraction delayed, moving a half-second slower than him. He blinked, glancing again, and it was normal. Just exhaustion. His mind was playing tricks on him.

The city lights loomed in the distance, but something about them seemed... different. Maybe dimmer, maybe too far away.

His vision wavered slightly, like heat rising from pavement. He blinked hard. It was just exhaustion. He had barely slept the past few nights. His mind was playing tricks on him.

He reached the hospital parking lot and barely remembered the turns he had taken to get there. He slammed the car door shut and ran inside, the sterile brightness of the hospital stinging his eyes. The hallway seemed too long, the overhead lights buzzing faintly. He told himself he was just dizzy from the rush.

Danny was there, pacing near the waiting area. He turned as Stewart approached, his face pale and drawn. "They're working on her," he said, rubbing a hand over his mouth. "She lost a lot of blood."

Stewart nodded, swallowing hard. His hands felt numb. The hallway behind Danny seemed to ripple for a brief second, like a heatwave distorting the air. He clenched his fists. His mind was playing tricks on him again. The stress. The anxiety. That's all it was.

He exhaled sharply and sat down, the chair beneath him feeling oddly weightless. The room felt colder now.

He rubbed his hands together, trying to ground himself. He was here. He had made it.

A doctor passed by, speaking in hushed tones to a nurse. Stewart caught snippets of the conversation: "...the body is still shifting...," "...we can't wake him up yet...," "...his mind isn't stabilizing..." The words barely made sense, dissolving into static in his head.

Danny sat beside him, rubbing his temples. "They're working on her," he muttered. Stewart nodded absently.

A few seconds passed. Then Danny repeated, in the exact same tone, "They're working on her."

Stewart blinked. "Yeah, you said that."

Danny didn't respond, just stared at the floor. His hands were still rubbing his temples, the same motion, the same pattern. For some reason, it unsettled Stewart, but he pushed the feeling aside. He was exhausted. His nerves were shot.

A nurse walked by, her footsteps oddly muffled against the tile floor. Stewart barely noticed as his eyelids grew heavier.

Then, just as his vision started to darken, he heard a voice—soft, yet firm. "Susan is in critical condition."

The room tilted. His breath caught in his throat. The words echoed inside his head, stretching, warping. His vision blurred, and before he could process anything, the world around him faded completely as he slumped forward, unconscious.

# 5

## The Cracks in Reality

———◦♡◦———

Stewart's eyes fluttered open, his breath hitching as the sterile white of the hospital ceiling came into focus. His body felt heavy, his limbs slow to respond. A dull ringing buzzed in his ears. He tried to sit up, but the moment he lifted his head, the world tilted violently.

Everything was spinning.

The walls stretched and twisted, the fluorescent lights above warping into spirals. The entire room rotated around him like a slow-moving carousel, and his stomach lurched. He gripped the sheets, his knuckles turning white. The motion wasn't just in his head—the whole world was moving.

"Stewart, hey, calm down."

Danny's voice cut through the haze. Stewart turned his head, barely making out Danny's face, but it wavered like a reflection on rippling water. Susan was there too, her hand resting gently on his arm, her expression etched with concern. But something about

them seemed off. Their voices had an echo, a slight distortion that made his skin prickle.

"Do you hear that?" Stewart's voice came out unsteady. "The room... it's moving."

Danny exchanged a glance with Susan. "You're probably just disoriented, man. You fainted. It's normal."

Normal? How was this normal? The walls rippled like liquid, the floor bending slightly beneath his weight. Stewart squeezed his eyes shut, taking slow, deep breaths. It had to be the stress, the anxiety. His mind was playing tricks on him. That's all it was.

After what felt like an eternity, the sensation dulled, the world steadying around him. His pulse slowed, though the unease still clawed at his gut.

"I need to get home," he muttered, swinging his legs over the bed.

Danny protested, but Stewart was already moving. He needed air, needed distance from whatever this was. The hospital walls pressed in too tight, and he couldn't shake the feeling that something was wrong.

The drive home was silent. Stewart's fingers gripped the wheel tighter than necessary, his mind still reeling from the episode. The roads stretched endlessly before him, the headlights cutting through the night. He exhaled, trying to shake the lingering dizziness. Maybe Danny was right. Maybe it was just stress.

Halfway home, a thought struck him like ice to the spine.

Susan was in critical condition.

His breath caught. Why was he driving home? Why had he left her at the hospital? Panic surged through him, his foot hovering over the brake. He needed to turn back. He had to see her.

His hands twisted the wheel sharply to make a U-turn, but his heart stopped mid-motion.

Susan and Danny were sitting in the back seat.

Stewart's throat tightened. His grip on the wheel trembled. He could see them clearly in the rearview mirror—Susan, pale but unharmed, and Danny, staring straight ahead, unblinking.

"That's not possible," he whispered. His breathing turned shallow. "You were just—"

Before he could finish, the road beneath them gave way.

The car lurched violently downward. His stomach flipped as the world tilted. The headlights cut through nothingness, illuminating only a gaping abyss below. Wind roared in his ears as gravity yanked them toward the cliffside. Panic slammed into him as he gripped the wheel, his instincts screaming to react.

He fought against the force pulling him down, yanking at the door handle, kicking against the frame. The seatbelt burned against his chest as he struggled. His fingers fumbled for something—anything—to grab onto. The air was thick, pressing in from all sides.

Then, with a violent jolt, he was free.

Stewart hit the ground hard, rolling onto the dirt as the car plummeted into the void. His breath came in ragged gasps, his body trembling. He scrambled to his feet, staring at the edge of the cliff where his car had just been.

Silence.

His pulse pounded in his ears. His hands ached from the impact, his legs unsteady. Slowly, he turned back.

Danny and Susan stood a few feet away, watching him.

Neither of them had moved from their spots in the car.

A cold chill crawled up his spine.

Something was terribly, terribly wrong.

# 6

## The Chaos Unfolds

Stewart gasped as he tumbled through the air, the wind screaming past his ears. One moment, he had been gripping the edge of the cliff, his car plunging into the abyss below—now, he was weightless, spiraling downward into a sky that wasn't supposed to be beneath him.

Then, he hit something—not with a crash, but with an unnatural softness, like sinking into thick fog. The sensation shifted, the ground beneath him solidifying into cracked asphalt. He staggered to his feet, realizing he was now standing in the middle of a burning city.

Flames licked at the sky, buildings crumbling into dust, yet he remained unharmed. A voice called his name.

"Stewart! What are you doing? Move!"

He spun around. Danny stood a few feet away, waving frantically. "The ground's about to give in!"

Stewart barely had time to process before the pavement cracked beneath his feet. He leaped instinctively onto a collapsed billboard that teetered on the shifting ground—just as the street caved into a river of molten lava.

"What the—" Stewart clutched the edge of the billboard as it floated across the lava like a makeshift raft.

Danny, now standing on a piece of debris somehow gliding alongside him, shrugged. "Weird, right?"

"Weird? WEIRD?" Stewart shouted. "None of this makes any damn sense!"

Danny only laughed, but his voice echoed unnaturally, repeating itself in layers. The sound sent a shiver down Stewart's spine.

The cityscape blurred and twisted, morphing into an ocean as high as the sky. The lava river had transformed into a massive wave that swallowed them whole. Stewart braced for the burning sensation—but there was none. Instead, he was floating, the water around him thickening, turning into glass, then shattering into a thousand tiny stars.

He crashed onto a beach—except the sand was made of paper, pages flipping as if an invisible wind was reading them. Susan was sitting on a chair nearby, reading a book titled *How to Survive the End of the World*.

She looked up and smirked. "Chapter 10 is really helpful. You should read it."

Stewart sat up, breathless. "Susan, what the hell is happening?"

She shrugged. "You tell me. You're the one dreaming."

His stomach dropped. "Dreaming?"

Before she could answer, the sky darkened. A shadow loomed overhead. Stewart looked up just in time to see an asteroid the size of a skyscraper plummeting straight toward them.

"RUN!" Danny's voice came from nowhere and everywhere at once.

Stewart turned to sprint, but the sand-paper pages tangled around his legs. He tripped, falling into a bottomless pit that hadn't been there before.

He screamed.

Then, silence.

Then—

A gentle breeze. The scent of rain. He opened his eyes to find himself standing in a meadow of floating islands, gravity shifting as if deciding where to place him next.

A deer with wings strolled past. It turned to him and said, "You're late."

Stewart groaned, rubbing his temples. "Of course I am."

The world flickered again, the ground tilting sideways. He lost his balance, tumbling into yet another impossible landscape. He landed in a subway car—except it wasn't underground. It was moving through the sky, cutting through storm clouds.

Passengers sat silently, all of them faceless. The intercom crackled.

"Next stop: Nowhere."

Stewart exhaled sharply. He was stuck in an ever-shifting nightmare, and the worst part?

Somewhere, deep down, he was starting to accept it.

—

A loud beep. The scent of antiseptic. A soft bed beneath him.

Stewart's eyes fluttered open. White walls, fluorescent lights humming softly. A hospital room.

His heart pounded with relief. It was over. The nightmare was over.

He exhaled sharply, letting his body sink into the bed. His hands trembled slightly, the last remnants of the dream fading from his mind. He was back. He was safe.

A shuffling noise. He turned his head, expecting to see a nurse or doctor.

Instead, he saw butchers. Their bloodstained aprons, their cold, dead eyes staring at him.

His breath hitched in his throat. His body tensed, panic surging through his veins.

One of them picked up a cleaver, testing its weight. Another sharpened a knife, the metallic scrape echoing through the sterile room.

His pulse roared in his ears. His limbs refused to move. He tried to scream, but no sound came out.

Somewhere, a voice whispered.

"Wake up. Wake up."

# 7
## Lost and Searching

—♡—

Danny gripped the steering wheel tightly as he and Susan pulled up to Stewart's house. His gut churned with unease. It had been two days, and Stewart hadn't answered a single call or text. That wasn't like him.

As they stepped up to the front door, they were surprised to find it already open. Inside, Melissa and James sat in the dimly lit living room, their expressions tight with concern.

"Where is he?" Danny asked immediately.

Melissa shook her head. "We don't know. He said he needed a break. That his dreams were getting... strange."

Susan's stomach twisted. "What do you mean strange?"

James rubbed his temples. "He wouldn't explain much. Just said they were becoming too real. That he was waking up still feeling trapped in them."

Melissa's voice was barely above a whisper. "He looked afraid. And then... he left."

Danny exchanged a glance with Susan. The words sent an eerie shiver through him. Stewart had always been open about his illness, but this sounded different.

"Did he say where he was going?" Susan pressed.

James shook his head. "No. But whatever he was running from, he believed it was chasing him."

A heavy silence filled the room.

Danny took a deep breath. "We need to check his room. Maybe he left something behind."

Upstairs, Stewart's room was in chaos. Papers were strewn across the desk, notebooks filled with frantic scribbles, his laptop still open. Susan scanned the notes, her fingers trembling.

"He was researching something about dreams again," she murmured, flipping through the pages. "And...look at this." She turned the laptop toward Danny. A list of locations, circled and underlined.

Danny frowned. "These are all remote. One of them's in the mountains."

Susan picked up a notebook, eyes widening as she read. "He told me he was having weird dreams... Ones that didn't feel like dreams at all."

Danny's expression darkened. "What do you mean?"

Susan swallowed hard. "He said they were getting worse. That he'd wake up and still feel like he was inside them. That the things in the dreams were watching him even after he woke up." She hesitated, her voice dropping to a whisper. "He said he needed to get away before they pulled him in for good."

A chill ran down Danny's spine. "What the hell does that mean?"

Susan shook her head. "I don't know. But he was scared. And now he's gone."

James stepped forward, scanning the notebook. "If he was tracking these locations, then he must have gone to one of them. We need to go now.

ᗺᗺᗺ

"The three of them drove into the mountains, following the markings Stewart had left

behind. Hours of searching finally led them to a remote trail, where they found Stewart collapsed near a ridge, unconscious but breathing.

Danny dropped to his knees beside him, shaking him gently. "Stewart! Can you hear me?"

No response. His skin was cool, his breathing shallow. Susan clutched his hand, her face pale with fear. James was already on the phone, calling for an ambulance.

When the paramedics arrived, they worked quickly, securing Stewart onto a stretcher and loading him into the ambulance. Danny and Susan sat inside while James rode in the front, his expression grim.

As they sped toward the hospital, James finally spoke. "You need to understand something. Stewart isn't just asleep. He's trapped."

Danny frowned. "What do you mean?"

James exhaled. "In a normal sleep cycle, when we die in a dream, we wake up. That's how the brain works. The dream ends, and we

return to reality. But Stewart... he's not in a normal sleep cycle. He's in an episode. If he dies in the dream, the dream will end—but he won't wake up. He'll go into a coma. His mind will be locked inside his own body."

Susan gasped. "So we can't wake him?"

James shook his head. "No one can. He has to survive until his episode naturally ends. If he doesn't... he may never come back."

A heavy silence filled the ambulance as the weight of James' words sank in.

When they finally reached the hospital, Stewart was rushed inside. The doctors monitored him closely, but they had no answers. Susan sat beside his bed, her hand wrapped around his, her face etched with worry.

She stared at him, willing him to wake up.

"Come back, Stewart," she whispered. "Please."

# 8

# The Dream Fights Back

Stewart sat on the beach, his fingers digging into the soft, warm sand. The waves rolled in with a rhythmic, soothing sound, and a golden sunset stretched across the horizon. It was peaceful—eerily so. The air smelled of salt and something faintly nostalgic, like a memory long forgotten.

Then, without warning, the sun flickered. It pulsed once, then again, its hue shifting from a warm yellow to a deep, menacing red. It expanded, growing larger in the sky, its light becoming uncomfortably bright. The temperature around him spiked.

Stewart squinted and shielded his eyes, his gut twisting with unease. Then he noticed something even worse—the ocean ahead of him was rising. Not in waves, but as an entire body. The horizon itself was *lifting*, as if the sea was tilting forward. The water didn't crest and break like a normal tsunami. Instead, it loomed, a vertical wall of deep, endless blue stretching high above him, swallowing the sky.

His breath hitched. His body screamed at him to *run*.

He scrambled to his feet, but his legs felt sluggish, the sand gripping at his ankles. The waterline drew closer, the air growing thick with pressure. His heartbeat pounded in his ears, a primal terror surging through him. He wasn't going to make it. The sea was about to consume him.

Then, from nowhere, a rope dropped in front of him. Thick and sturdy, it dangled from the sky, swaying as if beckoning him. There was no time to think—he grabbed it. The moment his fingers wrapped around the fibers, an unseen force yanked him upward. He ascended rapidly, the violent rush of wind whistling past his ears. The tsunami shrank below him, the monstrous wall of water folding into itself until it vanished completely.

Stewart gasped, clutching the rope as he broke through a thick layer of mist. Then, suddenly, he was standing—on clouds. The ground beneath his feet was soft and cool, the sky above stretching infinitely. It should have been beautiful, but something about it felt *wrong*.

A whisper drifted through the air.

"...Stewart... you're dreaming... wake up..."

His eyes widened. The voice was familiar. Distant. Warped, as though carried through water. It was Susan.

$$\triangleright\triangleright\triangleright$$

**Reality – The Hospital Room**

Susan gripped Stewart's hand tightly, her voice trembling. "Stewart, please. You have to wake up. You're dreaming."

Machines beeped erratically. His breathing had turned shallow, his body twitching as though struggling against something unseen. The doctors rushed in, checking the monitors, whispering to each other with tight, concerned expressions.

"His vitals are unstable," one muttered.

Danny paced in frustration, running a hand through his hair. "What the hell is happening to him? You guys said he was just in a deep sleep!"

James sat silently by the bed, watching Stewart intently. He had seen this before. He *knew* what was happening.

"He's fighting it," James murmured.

Danny turned to him. "Fighting what?!"

James didn't answer right away. He looked at his son's face—pale, damp with sweat, lips slightly parted as if trying to breathe through a nightmare. He had been in that place once, long ago. If Stewart didn't figure it out soon, the dream wouldn't just fight back—it would *swallow* him whole.

PPP

**Dream World**

The clouds beneath Stewart's feet darkened. The sky above flickered, like a dying lightbulb. The whisper came again, clearer this time, but fragmented—*"Stewart... dre...ming... wake..."*

He swayed, gripping his head. Why did Susan's voice sound so distant? Why did it feel like it was coming from *outside* of his world?

Then, a flicker of something—

A hospital room. Blurred figures hovering over a bed. Machines blinking. Someone gripping his hand.

His stomach lurched. *What was that?*

His own reflection rippled in the air before him, but it wasn't quite right—his eyes lagged, his mouth moved before sound came out. A terrible realization crawled into his mind like a parasite.

*This isn't real.*

The moment the thought registered, the dream fought back.

The rope vanished from his grasp. The clouds beneath him *shattered* into nothingness. A force yanked him downward, and he fell, spiraling into an endless abyss. The distorted echoes of Susan's voice faded into the darkness.

Stewart was drowning. Not in water, but in the weight of his own mind, dragging him deeper into the unknown.

# 9
# Lucid and Broken

A voice echoed through the air, distant and warped, like a whisper traveling across an ocean. Stewart turned his head, but there was no one there. The world around him—the darkened alleyway he had been walking through—began to shift subtly. The buildings stretched and then shrank, as if they were breathing. The streetlights flickered, their glow bending into unnatural shapes.

The voice came again. This time, clearer. **"Stewart... Wake up..."**

A shiver ran down his spine. The voice was familiar, yet wrong—distorted, stretched, as if spoken through a broken radio. He tried to focus. *Who was that?* The answer should have been obvious, but his mind felt sluggish, as though submerged in water.

His surroundings twisted again. The alleyway stretched into infinity before suddenly snapping back to its original size. Shadows warped unnaturally, flickering between shapes

that didn't belong. Stewart staggered back, breathing heavily.

Something was wrong.

His heart pounded as the realization clawed its way into his mind. He thought back to everything that had happened—the inconsistencies, the bizarre shifts, the events that made no sense. His pulse quickened. *This isn't real.*

Then it hit him like a crashing wave. **He was dreaming.**

A thrill rushed through him. He clenched his fist and imagined light bursting forth from his palm. Instantly, a glowing orb materialized, floating just above his fingers. His breath caught. *I can control it.*

He tested the limits—stretching his arm toward the sky, willing himself upward. The ground fell away beneath him, and he soared. The city below warped and reshaped as he directed it, bending to his will. He was no longer a prisoner of this world; he was its master.

Laughter bubbled in his chest. *This is incredible.* Buildings rose at his command, trees sprouted from the concrete, and the sky morphed into a swirling canvas of colors he had never seen before. Stewart grinned. *If I can control this place, I can escape it.*

But the moment the thought formed, the dream shifted.

The vibrant sky dimmed. The towering structures he had created trembled, then began to rot. The leaves on his newly formed trees blackened, curling inward like dying embers. The people in the streets—figures he hadn't paid much attention to—stopped moving. Their heads turned toward him in unison, their faces blank.

Stewart's exhilaration turned to dread. He willed the dream back to normal, but the more he struggled for control, the more unstable everything became. The sky cracked like shattered glass. The streets rippled like liquid. The faceless figures moved toward him, their movements unnatural, their limbs bending at angles that defied logic.

"No..." Stewart whispered. He tried to run, but his legs barely responded. The air around him thickened, pressing against him like an invisible weight. *I need to wake up.*

He squeezed his eyes shut and willed himself awake. Nothing happened. Panic set in. *Wake up. Wake up. WAKE UP.*

The faceless figures drew closer, whispering in voices that layered over one another, an incomprehensible symphony of madness. The dream was breaking apart, and so was he.

Then, the world collapsed.

It didn't explode or fade—it simply *ceased*. One moment, there was chaos. The next, there was nothing.

Pure, unending darkness.

Stewart opened his eyes—or at least, he thought he did. There was no light, no movement, no sound. He floated in the abyss, weightless and untethered. He tried to breathe but wasn't sure if he even had lungs anymore. His body, his world, his *self*—all of it had dissolved into nothingness.

A terrible realization dawned upon him.

He was trapped.

ÞÞÞ

**Meanwhile, in the Real World...**

The steady beeping of a heart monitor filled the hospital room. Susan gripped Stewart's hand, her knuckles white. Danny stood beside her, eyes locked onto the unmoving figure in the hospital bed.

"He's not responding," Danny muttered, voice strained with fear. "His vitals are dropping."

James took a slow, deep breath. "He's losing control," he murmured. "If he doesn't fight his way back, he might never wake up."

Susan's eyes welled with tears. She leaned down and whispered, her voice trembling but firm. **"Stewart... do anything. Don't let the dream consume you. Don't die until you naturally wake up."**

ϷϷϷ

**In the Dream World...**

Her voice cut through the abyss, distorted but still recognizable. Stewart heard her. A flicker of determination sparked in his chest. *I have to stay alive. I have to fight this.*

He focused, trying to reshape the void, trying to force something—anything—into existence. He summoned every ounce of willpower, calling forth light, movement, sound—

But the darkness only deepened.

The nothingness swallowed him whole.

# 10
## Trapped in the Void

Darkness. A vast, endless void stretching in all directions. Stewart's thoughts floated in it, weightless, disconnected, lost. Was this death? Had he finally succumbed? There was no sound, no form, just the presence of his own mind drifting in an abyss of nothingness. He screamed, but no voice came. He reached, but there was nothing to touch. He was alone.

Then, a flicker. A tiny ripple in the void. A distant beeping sound. The hum of fluorescent lights. A faint warmth on his skin.

Vision returned in a blur—shadows, indistinct shapes above him. His ears rang as sounds sharpened, voices overlapping in a mix of muffled panic and medical precision. Stewart's gaze fixed on the ceiling, sterile white, lined with soft, buzzing lights. He was in a hospital room.

Relief surged through him—he was alive.

But when he tried to move, nothing happened.

A cold wave of fear crawled through him. He tried again. No response. His arms, his legs, his fingers—nothing obeyed. His mouth remained closed, silent. He was awake inside his own body, trapped.

Then came the voices.

The door opened. Footsteps approached, shoes tapping against the tile floor. He recognized the tone before the words registered—the clinical detachment of a doctor.

"He has slipped into a coma," the neurospecialist announced. "His brain activity is minimal. We will continue monitoring, but there's no indication of responsiveness."

No. That wasn't true. He was here. He could hear them. He was awake!

A broken sob filled the room. His mother. "Please... he's still in there, right?" Her voice cracked as if she was afraid of the answer.

"I'm sorry," the doctor replied gently. "At this stage, we have to consider the possibility of no recovery."

No. NO! Stewart wanted to scream, to prove them wrong, to move, to blink, to do anything. He focused all his energy on his hand. Just one twitch. One motion. His body remained lifeless.

His father's voice came next, calm but heavy. "What... what do we do now?"

"There are options," the doctor said. "We can keep him on life support, but in cases like this, it's also an option to consider letting the patient pass peacefully."

His mother gasped. "You're telling us to let our son die?"

A sharp scrape of a chair. Footsteps. The door opening, then shutting abruptly. Danny had left. Stewart could almost see him, standing in the hospital hallway, fists clenched, trying to process the shock.

Susan didn't move. He heard her crying softly beside him. He longed to hold her, to tell her he was still here. But he was powerless.

Days passed. Or maybe hours. Time blurred in the prison of his own body. He had no choice but to live inside his memories.

Danny's laugh, loud and shameless, as they mocked each other's awful taste in music. Late-night drives with no destination. The freedom of youth, the ease of it all. He remembered the day they skipped class just to watch an old sci-fi marathon at Danny's house, eating junk food and arguing about plot holes. He could almost hear Danny's voice, teasing him, making ridiculous theories about time travel. It felt so real.

Susan's smile during their first coffee date. The way her eyes crinkled when she laughed. The nervous way she stirred her drink even when she wasn't adding anything to it. The hours they spent in that quiet little café, talking about dreams, fears, and the future. He remembered how she absentmindedly drew tiny patterns in the condensation on her cup, how her fingers lingered near his on the table. It was the moment he realized he never wanted to be without her.

His father's voice, steady and guiding, teaching him how to ride a bike. His mother's soft lullabies from a time when monsters were only in his imagination, not in his reality. The warm scent of home-cooked meals, the laughter around the dinner table, the small moments he never thought twice about before—but now, they were everything.

This was all he had now. The past.

And the present? It was slipping away. He heard more discussions. More hesitation. More pleas. The doctors were pushing his family toward a decision.

Then, the moment came. He watched them all, his family, his love, his best friend. He memorized their faces, knowing this was the last time he would see them.

His gaze drifted around the room, taking in the medical machines, the IVs, the sterile walls. He needed to know how long he had been here, how long he had been gone.

His eyes landed on the calendar.

A simple thing. Neatly placed on the wall. But something about it struck him.

He knew that calendar.

It was familiar. Too familiar.

A chill ran through his trapped body. His mind sharpened, cutting through the haze of

helplessness. A memory surfaced, fast and sudden.

"Wait a minute."

Darkness shifted. Awareness surged. Something was wrong.

# 11
## Final Awakening

The calendar.

Stewart's mind clung to it, desperate to remember. He knew it. He had seen it before. But where? The answer lurked in his memories, just beyond reach. He pushed himself deeper, further, searching through the fog of his past.

His childhood.

A flood of memories rushed in. The cozy living room of his old house, the worn-out couch where he would sit for hours, the glow of the bulky old TV that stood proudly against the wall. And above it—there it was. The same calendar. Hanging there for years, unchanged, marking time in a world that once felt endless.

He remembered the simple joys of childhood. Running home from school, throwing his bag aside, and jumping onto the couch. He and Danny would argue over which cartoon to watch first—*Tom and Jerry* or *Ben 10*. They'd mimic the characters, laughing until their stomachs hurt. No smartphones, no distractions, just the pure thrill of waiting for the next episode to air.

Weekends meant gaming marathons with Danny, their eyes glued to the screen as they battled in *Street Fighter* or raced in *Need for Speed: Most Wanted*. The frustration of losing, the victory dances when they won—it was all so vivid. School holidays felt like a lifetime of freedom, with no worries except for which ice cream to pick from the street vendor outside.

And Susan—his first crush, his first date. He could almost feel the nervous excitement of that evening, the way his hands trembled as he held his coffee cup. How they had talked for hours, losing track of time, discovering each other in a way that felt so effortless, so real.

A soft smile formed in his mind. This calendar had brought all of it back. He felt... alive. But then—

Wait.

Something was wrong.

He focused on the calendar again, his vision still blurry, struggling to see the numbers clearly. And then he saw it—the date.

It wasn't today's date. It wasn't from this year. It was from his childhood. The numbers stared back at him, frozen in time, untouched by reality.

His breath caught. His thoughts sharpened.

"I'm dreaming."

He forced himself to say it in his mind, over and over. *I'm dreaming. This isn't real. I need to wake up. I have to wake up.* He pushed with every ounce of strength, willing his body to move. His fingers twitched—just barely.

He didn't stop. He wouldn't stop.

More force. More will. His hand lifted, trembling, breaking through the paralysis. A surge of triumph filled him. He reached out, grabbing Susan's hand beside him, gripping it tightly.

With a rush of emotions, he turned towards his father, his heart pounding with joy. He reached for him, wanting nothing more than to see his face, to let him know he was still here.

And then—

The world shattered.

The hospital room dissolved, peeling away like paper in the wind. The walls crumbled, the floor vanished. Stewart was weightless, floating, falling. Stars stretched around him, endless and breathtaking. Galaxies spiraled, nebulae burned with cosmic fire, the vast infinity of space unfolding before his eyes.

A voice. Deep. Ancient. Terrifying.

"So, you finally understand."

The words echoed through the void, sending tremors through Stewart's very being. A presence loomed before him, massive and overwhelming. He lifted his head, and his breath caught in his throat.

A towering figure stood before him, cloaked in swirling shadows darker than the void itself. Its form was skeletal yet unnervingly alive, its hollow eyes burning with an eerie, endless glow. Wisps of black mist coiled around its limbs like living smoke. When it moved, the universe itself seemed to tremble.

Death.

The entity stared down at him, its gaze heavy with knowing. "You are stubborn," it said. "But now, you have control."

Stewart felt something in his hand. He looked down.

A sword. Pure white, glowing with an ethereal light so brilliant it cast away the surrounding darkness. It pulsed in his grip, radiating power. It was small compared to the being before him—insignificant, almost laughable.

And yet, Stewart tightened his grip.
Because he was ready.

# Take a Break

Take a break, you are far too excited, go out and feel the fresh air, you have to sit and finish the climax now

# 12

# The Final Confrontation

The battle against Death raged on in the vast, empty expanse of space. A single platform, floating amidst the void, served as their battleground—a creation of Death itself. The stars flickered in the distance, cold and uncaring, mirroring the presence of the entity before him.

Stewart stood, sword in hand, his breaths heavy and labored. His body ached, his mind spiraled, but he forced himself to focus. His lucid control wavered, the sword in his grip shifting—at times feeling weightless, at others impossibly heavy.

Death, a towering figure draped in shifting darkness and light, regarded him with a gaze that felt both detached and deeply knowing. It had no fixed form—at moments, it was humanoid, at others, an abstract force of ever-changing matter. Yet its presence was undeniable. Unshakable.

"You struggle," Death observed, its voice calm yet echoing in the abyss, laced with something indecipherable. Not mockery, not pity—something in between. "You lash out as if striking the unknown will grant you understanding."

Stewart didn't answer. He lunged, slashing his sword in a precise arc, but Death merely tilted its head. The moment the blade should have struck, the space around it twisted. The platform beneath his feet distorted, shifting momentarily into a memory—his childhood home—before reverting to the battleground.

Stewart staggered, gripping his head as a sharp pain shot through him. He knew he was dreaming, but the shift was too disorienting. Too real.

Death stepped forward. "You wield your weapon, yet it falters. Why?"

The sword flickered in his hands, its once-sharp edge dulling. Stewart grit his teeth, gripping it tighter, forcing his will into the blade. It steadied, but only barely.

Death's form pulsed, and with a mere movement, the battlefield fractured. The space around them became an endless hallway lined with mirrors, each reflection showing Stewart in different forms—older, younger, victorious, defeated. A thousand versions of himself, yet he remained lost.

"You seek to fight me," Death continued, voice weaving through the mirrors, "but tell me, do you even know what you fight for?"

Stewart charged again, shattering the illusions with a sweep of his sword. The mirrors collapsed into dust, revealing the void once more. He panted, sweat forming despite the cold emptiness.

Death merely watched. "You are lost, Stewart. That is why you fail."

His grip on the sword wavered. No. He couldn't let it get to him. He was lucid. He was in control.

Wasn't he?

Death took another step forward. "You persist in a battle you have already lost."

Stewart roared, swinging with all his might. This time, his blade struck something—but instead of resistance, he felt his weapon phase through Death like smoke. Before he could react, the force of his own attack was thrown back at him, sending him hurtling across the battlefield.

He crashed onto the ground, gasping. His body felt heavier than before, his thoughts slower. His confidence cracked.

Death's presence loomed over him. "You misunderstand, Stewart. I do not need to defeat you. You are doing that yourself."

Stewart tried to rise, but his limbs felt like lead. His sword, once a part of him, lay beside him, dim and useless.

He clenched his fists. No. He had to win. He had to...

Death knelt beside him, voice barely above a whisper. "Tell me... what is it you truly fear?"

The world flickered again, distorting. The battlefield melted into something else entirely—a hospital room, sterile and quiet. His own body lay in the bed, unconscious, wires attached to his skin. A heart monitor beeped steadily, indifferent to his struggle.

A suffocating dread filled him. This wasn't real. It couldn't be.

But Death's voice persisted. "You are slipping, Stewart."

The room vanished. He was back on the battlefield, on his knees, shaking.

Death stood tall, silent.

Stewart gritted his teeth, trying to force himself back into control. He raised his sword once more.

Death did not move. It did not need to.

The battle had already been decided.

And Stewart had lost.

Silence hung heavy between them. The vastness of space swallowed the sound of Stewart's ragged breaths. His sword, which had once gleamed with potential, now felt like a foreign object in his hands. He wanted to fight. He had to fight. But what was the point?

Death began to circle him slowly, its movements fluid, effortless. "You misunderstand something fundamental, Stewart. You believe that this is a battle you can win. That there is a path forward where you emerge victorious."

Stewart remained silent, watching as Death's form shifted—briefly, it became a towering shadow, then something smaller, more human, a figure from his past he couldn't quite place. It was playing with him, warping the dream, warping his mind.

Death suddenly stopped. "Your father was here once."

Stewart's breath caught.

"Yes," Death continued, almost amused. "He stood where you stood. He fought, just as you do now. He failed, just as you are failing."

Stewart's grip tightened. "No... he's alive."

"For now." Death's voice darkened. "Do you think he escaped me? No. The dream ended before I could claim him. A temporary reprieve, nothing more. But he learned something that you have not."

The platform beneath Stewart's feet shifted, revealing an abyss of infinite blackness below. "He learned never to wake himself up before achieving his purpose. You, however... you will not have that luxury."

Death gestured toward the void. "Do you see it? That empty pit? It is not an escape. It is where you will remain if you fail. No light. No sound. Just you, forever, calling for help that will never come."

Stewart's heartbeat pounded in his ears.

"Do you understand now?" Death whispered, its presence pressing against him. "You do not have two options. You have only one. You will either defeat me... or you will fall into the abyss. But make no mistake, Stewart."

Death leaned in, its voice turning to ice. "I will not lose. Nor will I allow you to escape."

The battlefield grew dim. The stars in the distance flickered, then vanished. The platform beneath him cracked, splintering into nothingness. Space itself seemed to collapse inward, consuming him.

Stewart's mind screamed at him to fight, to resist, but his body—his very will—betrayed him.

As the last remnants of the battlefield dissolved into the void, Death's voice was the only thing that remained.

"Rest now, Stewart."

And then, there was nothing.

# 13
## The Abyss of Understanding

Stewart drifted in the void, his breath shallow, his body weightless. The remnants of his shattered sword floated beside him, fading into the endless black. His hands trembled, gripping at nothing. He had fought with everything he had, bending the very fabric of this dream world to his will, yet Death stood before him, unchanged, unwavering.

Death did not move. It no longer swung its weapon nor pressed forward with an attack. Instead, it merely watched him, silent and patient, as if waiting for Stewart to come to a realization of his own.

A cold shiver ran through him. "Why aren't you finishing this?" he asked, his voice hoarse.

Death tilted its head, the void beneath its hood shifting like a chasm without end. "Because you have not yet understood."

Stewart clenched his fists. "Understood what? That I'm weak? That I can't win?" He spat the words out, frustration mounting. His entire body ached, his mind frayed at the edges. His lucid control had failed him. His sword had failed him. And now, he was left with nothing but himself. "I've fought. I've done everything I can. What else is there?"

Death took a step closer, but there was no menace in its movements—only an unfathomable certainty. "Winning was never the goal."

Stewart's breath caught in his throat. "Then what was?"

A long silence stretched between them before Death finally spoke. "Tell me, Stewart. What do you fear most?"

He felt the weight of the question press down on him. In the deepest corners of his mind, he knew the answer. It wasn't Death itself. It wasn't losing this fight. It was something more terrifying, more absolute.

"I... I fear never waking up," he admitted, the words shaking him to his core. "I fear being trapped here forever."

Death's form flickered, the darkness around it pulsing. "Then tell me, what does it mean to wake up?"

The question rattled him more than any battle ever could. What *did* it mean to wake up? He had always assumed it was about opening his eyes, feeling his body, returning to reality. But was that truly waking up? Or was there something more?

The dream had fought him at every turn. The landscapes had twisted, the people had lied, and even now, standing before Death itself, he felt as though he were missing the most important piece of the puzzle.

His breathing steadied. The void around him rippled. He looked down at his own hands, and for the first time, they seemed less solid. Less real.

"This world... it's mine, isn't it?" he whispered. "I've been fighting it, trying to force it to obey me, but that was never the way. I don't have to control it. I have to *understand* it."

A slow, deliberate nod came from Death. "And so, what will you do now?"

Stewart exhaled. For so long, he had resisted, trying to conquer what could not be conquered. But now he saw the truth. If he wanted to wake up, he had to stop fighting.

With nothing left to lose, he let go.

The moment he surrendered, the battlefield of space crumbled into darkness. Death faded, its presence neither hostile nor welcoming. The dreamworld collapsed, folding into itself, pulling Stewart downward.

And then—

He was sitting by a beautiful sea, the golden light of the setting sun painting the waves in hues of amber and crimson. The salty breeze brushed against his skin, gentle, familiar. He looked to his side, and there, standing beside him, was Death.

But it was no longer a towering, faceless entity. It had taken human form—a calm presence, neither ominous nor threatening. Its eyes held no malice, only understanding.

"You have spent so much time resisting," Death said, its voice smooth and knowing. "When you first found out about the disease you could not cure, you resisted. You resisted sleep. You resisted being the person you were in childhood. You tried to control it, command it, even defeat it—but you never accepted it."

Stewart's throat tightened. He had never put it into words, but he knew it was true.

Death continued, "Now, you have finally found your truth. You will wake up now."

The dream began to fall apart, dissolving like sand slipping through his fingers. The sea, the sky, the breeze—all fading. And in their place, something new emerged.

A hospital room.
The beeping of monitors.
Blurry figures standing over him.
Susan. Danny. Melissa. James.
His family. His friends. His reality.
He was finally awake.

# 14
## Awakening

The world was collapsing.

Stewart felt it—his surroundings breaking apart, the very fabric of his dream unraveling like threads being pulled from a worn tapestry. The sky darkened, the ground beneath him cracked, and the air vibrated with an eerie hum, as if the entire world was letting out a final breath.

He was running, but he didn't know where. Every step felt heavier, his limbs burdened by exhaustion. The figures he had met—the ones who had guided him, challenged him, and even tried to destroy him—were fading into nothingness. Their voices, once so real, now echoed like distant memories.

Something was pulling him, not with force, but with inevitability.

His mind, his body, his soul—it all screamed for release.

Then, the world shattered.

A sharp inhale.

Stewart's eyes flew open, his lungs burning as he gasped for air. The ceiling above him was familiar—too familiar. White. Sterile. The rhythmic beeping of a heart monitor filled the silence, grounding him in a reality he had almost forgotten.

He was awake.

The weight of his body pressed into the hospital bed, the stiffness of his muscles a testament to how long he had been lying there. The room smelled of antiseptic and something faintly floral—lilies. His mother's favorite. His heart pounded as he turned his head to the side.

Melissa sat by his bedside, her hands clasped together, her eyes swollen and red-rimmed. When their gazes met, she let out a choked sob, covering her mouth as if afraid the sound might break the fragile moment.

"Stewart," she whispered, voice trembling.

His lips parted, but no words came. He swallowed, the dryness in his throat making it painful. "Mom..."

A gasp, then a flurry of movement. The chair scraped back as she rushed to him, grasping his hand between hers, warm and shaking. Tears spilled freely down her cheeks as she nodded, as if reassuring herself that this was real, that he was real.

James was there too. Stewart saw him standing in the doorway, his father's usually composed face breaking with emotion. He stepped forward, hesitated, then placed a firm hand on Stewart's shoulder. "Welcome back, son."

The weight of those words hit him harder than he expected.

Back.

He was back.

His mind swirled with everything that had transpired in the dream—so vivid, so real. He had lived another life, fought battles, felt fear, love, loss. And yet... none of it existed in this world. It was a fragment of his mind, a place he had been trapped within for what felt like an eternity.

"W-what... how long?" Stewart croaked.

Melissa sniffled, brushing his hair back with gentle fingers. "It's been nearly six months."

Six months.

The words sank into him, a weight heavier than he was prepared to bear. He had been asleep, lost in a world of his own creation, for half a year. The dream had stretched far longer than that—years, maybe more. And yet, here he was. Awake. Alive.

Tears burned at the back of his eyes, though he wasn't sure why. Relief? Fear? Grief for something that had never truly existed?

His mother kissed his forehead, murmuring soft reassurances he couldn't quite process. His father squeezed his shoulder once more before stepping out, likely to call for a doctor. The beeping of the monitor continued steadily, its rhythm a quiet reminder that his heart was still beating, his body still functioning.

ᗡᗡᗡ

A week later, Stewart was finally home. The house felt the same, yet somehow different—like returning after a long journey. He was still adjusting, still processing what had happened, but he wasn't alone.

Danny and Susan arrived later that evening, their faces lighting up the moment they saw him.

"Man, you really took beauty sleep to a whole new level," Danny quipped, shaking his head with a chuckle.

Stewart huffed a laugh, feeling warmth spread through him. "Yeah, I guess I overdid it."

Susan crossed her arms, though her eyes shimmered with relief. "I was worried sick about you, you idiot. Six months? Do you have any idea how much I stressed over you?"

"Trust me, I think I have an idea," Stewart said with a small smile.

Danny grinned. "Well, at least you're back to your usual sarcastic self. That's a good sign."

Melissa laughed, shaking her head. "I swear, the three of you never change."

James chuckled, placing a reassuring hand on Stewart's shoulder. "And that's how it should be."

For the first time in what felt like forever, Stewart allowed himself to let go of the weight he had been carrying. The dream was over, but life was still here, waiting for him.

And he was ready to live it.

The room filled with laughter, warmth, and the unmistakable sense of home.

Stewart was finally, truly awake.

# Thank You

Writing The Dreamer's Abyss has been a journey of diving into the unconscious, of wrestling with dreams and surfacing with stories. To those who supported me through this surreal plunge—thank you.

To the dreamers, the night thinkers, and the people who understood Stewart before he understood himself—your encouragement kept this world alive.

To the researchers and communities who've shared insights into Kleine-Levin Syndrome, your knowledge helped ground the fantastical in something real.

To my beta readers and friends who asked the hard questions and pushed me to go deeper: this story is stronger because of you.

And finally, to you, the reader—thank you for taking the leap into the abyss.

# About The Author

Sunil K writes stories where reality bends, time folds, and the line between consciousness and dream blurs. Fascinated by altered states of mind, unexplainable phenomena, and the untold power of memory, they aim to explore the unknown with every page.

When not writing, they're probably questioning time travel mechanics, chasing storms, or getting lost in sci-fi films and metaphysical thought experiments.

The Dreamer's Abyss is their debut novel.

# A Final Word

If The Dreamer's Abyss resonated with you, unsettled you, or left you somewhere between asleep and awake—I've done my job.

We all drift sometimes.
We all dream.
And maybe, just maybe, the dream dreams back.

— Sunil K